Not in a
Thousand
Years

Story by Louise Schofield
Illustrations by Liz Alger

Contents

Chapter One

Marg, Pop, and Monster

I must be the only kid in the world who thinks that visiting your grandparents is the most exciting thing you can do on your school vacations. But then, I'm the only person I know who has grandparents like mine.

Marg and Pop are different from everyone else I know. Sometimes I think they're a bit crazy, but they're THE BEST, and occasionally, I wish I lived with them all the time.

This time Marg and Pop were taking me camping. They had promised to show me something extra special. It was going to be great fun! I couldn't wait...

Marg and Pop were waiting at the station when my train pulled in. You couldn't miss them. As usual, Marg was wearing the most amazing clothes. This time she wore one of her "ready-for-anything" safari suits. Not only was the color funny, but she had so many gadgets hanging off her belt, you'd think she was ready for battle.

Pop was wearing an old station-master's cap from his famous hat collection. He likes to wear a different hat every day. Mom calls him the Mad Hatter.

Marg and Pop's dog, Monster, was there as well. As usual, he was excited to see me.

"Monster, you mad dog, I'm back!"

When Monster had finished licking me to death, we piled into Marg and Pop's truck and headed for town to buy supplies for the camping trip. We needed lots of food.

"Choose anything you like, Jack," said Marg, grinning — she knew I had a bit of a sweet tooth.

At the butcher, I picked out hot dogs and chicken. At the supermarket, I picked out chocolate, cookies, cakes, and some fruit, too.

Pop selected a huge watermelon, the size of a dinosaur egg.

"You always need a big watermelon when you go camping," he said, giving me a wink.

Next stop was Marg and Pop's farm. I never knew how we were going to get there — Marg always drove and she never liked to drive the same way twice in one week. She said that was boring.

Sometimes the trip to the farm would be quick and direct, and other times it would take hours while Marg drove along back roads, through small lanes, and over forgotten bridges.

But today Marg took her favorite short-cut. It was an interesting ride!

That night, after dinner, we played cards. We had a great time, but every now and then Pop would look at me and smile like a Cheshire Cat.

"You'll never guess what our surprise will be, Jack," he said with a wink. "Not in a *thousand* years."

"Now, don't go giving him hints, dear," said Marg.

When I went to bed, I couldn't sleep for wondering what the surprise would be. But I knew they'd *never* tell me. I would just have to wait.

Chapter Two

Meeting Alice

I woke when George the rooster crowed, just as the sun was coming up. I didn't need an alarm at Marg and Pop's — although sometimes I wished I could turn George off! After breakfast, we packed our camping gear in a trailer attached to the truck and headed off.

Monster sat at the back of the truck, his head hanging over the side. He loved going on adventures with Marg and Pop — nearly as much as I did.

At the last stop, before heading off the main road to our campsite, we bought ice cream. Even Monster had one!

But then, much to my surprise, we left Monster with a friend of Pop's and waved good-bye.

"Why did we have to leave Monster behind?" I asked, as the truck bumped its way up a rough trail. Marg looked at me in the rear mirror, smiling.

"You'll find out in good time."

We drove over rocky, rough trails, through floodways, and even over some sand. We became bogged down once, but Pop and I laid sticks and small branches over the muddy trail so the tires could get a grip. Easy!

We finally arrived at a place that I'd never been before. A large sign told me we were entering a national park. No wonder we couldn't bring Monster — no dogs allowed! But what Marg and Pop's surprise might be, I couldn't be sure. A giant tree to climb? A rare animal? I'd have to wait and see.

We made camp in a clearing by a creek. A big hill with lots of fantastic boulders and rocks loomed over us from the other side. Pop and I put up the two tents while Marg made a fire.

Just as we put a pot of water on the fire to boil, a national park ranger drove up. Marg and Pop seemed to have been expecting her. Her name was Alice and she joined us for a cup of coffee and a piece of Pop's fruitcake.

Alice and my grandparents sounded like they were talking in code. Alice was obviously in on "the surprise," and they were all smiling at me and nodding. By now I was getting a bit annoyed at being the only one left out.

"See you in a couple of days, Jack," said Alice before she drove off. "You're in for quite a treat!"

After she left, Pop suggested we go exploring.

Chapter Three

Crazy Games — But No End to the Secret

The creek near the campsite was full of little fish, and every now and then, Pop and I found a frog among the rocks and reeds. In places, the creek rushed over rocks like mini-rapids; in other places it slowed to become a quiet pond.

I made a tiny raft out of twigs, using reeds as twine, and watched it head off on an exciting journey. Then Pop decided to liven things up.

"Let's play follow-the-leader!"

Pop scampered over a fallen log — and I followed. Then he began hopping from rock to rock in the creek. I hopped after him.

We were having a great time — and I was starting to catch up with him — when suddenly Pop said, "Uh-oh!"

A rock was wobbling... Pop was wobbling...

He waved his arms madly, one leg in the air, and... *SPLASH!*

Pop fell in.

I went to rescue him and... *SPLASH!* I fell in, too.

We sat in the creek laughing so much that Marg came to see what the commotion was about. She had her camera with her.

"Smile, boys!"

We smiled!

After Pop and I dried off, Marg brought out a pair of binoculars. I lay in a hammock that Marg had hung between two trees and spied on anything that came in sight. I saw lots of colorful birds, swooping and chasing each other in the sunlight.

Later, I helped Pop cook our dinner. We barbecued hot dogs and onions and ate them with bread and salad. For dessert, we wrapped bananas in foil and put them on the edge of the hot coals until they were cooked. We served them with whipped cream and sprinklings of brown sugar. Delicious!

That night, when I crawled into my sleeping bag and was alone with my thoughts, I tried to guess what the surprise could be.

A waterfall? A pit full of snakes? I was running out of ideas.

"Goodnight, Jack. Don't stay awake trying to guess our surprise!" called Marg from the other tent.

"You'll never guess … not even in a *million* years," said Pop, with a chuckle. He did like to rub it in.

But they needn't have worried. I was so tired that even Pop's snoring couldn't keep me awake.

Chapter 4

Whispering in the Night

On our first morning at camp, Pop showed me how to fly fish for trout. Trout fishermen use a special fishing rod with a thick, nylon line and an artificial lure that looks like a flying insect. You've got to flick the line in and out in a special way, and then land it on the water, just like a bug might land.

If you're lucky, there will be a hungry trout waiting under a rock ledge.

Unfortunately we didn't catch anything, but we had a lot of fun trying.

For the rest of the day we swam in the creek, played cards, and read books. And that night, we went looking for nocturnal animals. Marg handed me a flashlight that had a strong beam. We walked quietly through the woods, listening and watching, shining the flashlight up and down the trees. If there were any nocturnal animals in the trees, their eyes would shine brightly in the light. Marg said some nocturnal animals have special eyes so they can see better in the dark.

We saw some possums, and an owl with two owlets on the branches of a big, old tree.

After our walk, we sat around the campfire, and Pop told me ghost stories while we sipped hot chocolate and toasted marshmallows. He reckoned the stories were true — and seemed to be getting scared himself just telling them — but Marg didn't look convinced.

Neither Marg nor Pop mentioned the surprise today, but it didn't stop me from thinking about it. When I went to bed, I could hear them whispering in the dark.

Unfortunately, I couldn't understand what they were saying.

Chapter Five

Day of Surprises

After breakfast, Marg and Pop said they were taking me for a long trek, and we wouldn't be back until the end of the day. We made sandwiches, filled bottles with water, and put on plenty of sun screen. I could tell by the way they were smiling and joking that today was *the day*. Soon, I would see the surprise.

Before we left camp, we put the fire out with sand and zipped up our tents to keep the animals out. We didn't want to come back to find snakes in our sleeping bags!

Marg, Pop, and I followed the creek upstream, crossed over a fallen log bridge to the other side, and began climbing the hill.

The hill was steep and the sun was warm. Marg led the way, while Pop and I took it more slowly, stopping every now and then to turn around and admire the view.

We passed many amazing rocks. Some of them were shaped like faces, while others were balanced as if the wind might blow them down the hill at any moment. Tiny flowers grew out of stony cracks.

Pop found the perfect place to sit, a royal throne carved out of stone. Pop and I stopped for a while until Marg called to us to hurry up!

Pop and I soon joined Marg on the hilltop. We had the most amazing view. You could see in all directions — 360 degrees — and it was fantastic! For a moment I thought the view was the surprise, but when I looked at Marg and Pop, I knew that the hilltop was just a wonderful place to take a rest. Marg handed me some water and a chocolate cookie.

Suddenly Marg called out, "An eagle!"

She pointed high into the sky.

Marg handed me the binoculars. I'd never seen an eagle before — it was beautiful! I couldn't believe how big it was. Looking through the binoculars, I could clearly see its sharp, curved beak. Marg said that really big eagles have a wingspan of nearly nine feet.

"Awesome!"

Eventually the eagle glided away, out of sight. I knew I'd seen something really special and couldn't wait to tell my friends back home.

"Wow!" I said. "That was a *great* surprise!"

Marg and Pop looked at each other and laughed.

"That was special," said Pop, "but that wasn't *our* surprise."

Suddenly I heard someone calling, "COO-EEE!"

Pop looked at Marg and smiled that secretive smile again.

"It's time to move on."

Marg stood up and turned to where the cry had come from. She called back, "COO-EEE!" She was signaling to someone, and I started to feel very excited. The eagle was fantastic, but what could be better? I'd been waiting for this for ages!

We listened to the COO-EEEs and followed them down the other side of the hill. I soon saw Alice, standing on a rocky ledge, waving at me. We wound our way around the hill and along a small trail to where she stood.

When we got there, Alice had mysteriously disappeared. Then Marg pushed past some bushes. I couldn't believe what I saw …

Chapter Six

A Very Special Place

"Wow!"

Hidden behind the bushes was an entrance
to a large cave. Alice stood in the cave's mouth,
waiting for us. She wore a hard hat and was
holding a large flashlight. Three more protective
hats lay at her feet.

We put the hats on and entered the cave.
The stone walls were smooth from water that
had once traveled through there millions of
years ago. In places, the walls looked smoky, as
if fires had once been lit inside the cave.
Daylight still lit up the area of the cave where
we stood, but the back of the cave disappeared
into inky blackness.

"You're very lucky, Jack," Alice began. "Very few people know about this place, but because Marg and Pop are my friends — and they wanted to treat you to something extra special — I'm going to show you something you'll remember for a long, long time."

My heart thumped. What could it be?

"I want all of you to stay close to me — don't wander off. We don't need to go far in, but you must always be careful in caves. Marg, did you bring your flashlight?"

Marg pulled it out of her backpack and turned it on.

"Right. Let's go!"

We headed into the darkness, our flashlights lighting our way. I felt the air turn cold and damp. I heard the *drip, drip, drip* of water. And then something squeaked!

Marg pointed her flashlight at the cave ceiling. Suddenly bats were everywhere! Before we knew what was happening, hundreds of them flapped and flitted around us, squealing.

I screamed! Pop shouted! Marg started yelling, and Alice called for calm!

"They'll be gone soon," she said.

Thankfully, the bats headed out of the cave the way we had come in, and disappeared.

For a moment, I thought my heart had stopped from shock, but my feet were still moving, so I figured I was all right. It was very dark now and the cave walls seemed to be closing in. I felt a bit scared, but then saw a bright light ahead.

The cave suddenly opened out again and sunlight poured in from high above us.

"Wow!"

In this eerie cave, deep in the earth, we'd come to a *very* special place. Along the cave walls were handprints and strange paintings of animals and people. The paintings looked really old, like something I'd seen in a book.

Pop put his hand on my shoulder, as if to say, "Well, Jack, this is our surprise!" But no words came out. He was speechless, just like me.

Finally Alice's voice broke the silence, but she spoke slowly and quietly.

"These are the paintings left behind by people who lived and hunted in this area *thousands* of years ago."

The hairs on the back of my neck prickled, listening to those words. Suddenly, I felt really cold. I shivered.

"These people might have been my ancestors," Alice continued. "My people come from around here and have stories about this country and its animals.

"Here on the walls, you can see pictures of men and women and the animals they used to hunt and eat."

Alice then explained how the paint had been made from different clays and ground-up stone and ash.

It was incredible. We were standing where prehistoric people had stood thousands of years ago. Alice said they had probably slept there, too, and cooked near the front of the cave. The smoke on the cave walls was probably from their fires.

We stayed for a long time looking at the paintings, wondering about the people who had once been here, painting their pictures.

The air of the cave seemed heavy... heavy with history and something else. Maybe it was my imagination (I couldn't be sure) but I thought I heard whispering, the whispering of ancient voices...

Chapter Seven

Things I'll Always Remember

When it was time to leave the cave, we thanked Alice for showing us this special place.

"It was *amazing*," I told her. "I'll never forget this place — ever."

Then Marg, Pop, and I trekked back to camp. The climb down the hillside was easier, but Pop and I still needed to stop at our rocky throne for a rest and a drink.

For the whole way back to camp, I couldn't stop thinking about what I had just seen. But somehow — out in the fresh air and the warm sunshine — it just seemed like an incredible dream.

When we got back to camp I was so hungry I could have eaten a dinosaur egg — but we hacked open the watermelon instead. It was juicy and sweet, and just what we needed after such an adventure.

Then I sat on a rock in the creek, cooling my feet. I took a big bite of watermelon and thought of something else that I would remember forever ... Pop was right! You *always* need a big watermelon when you go camping!